Dear Reader,

I, Nate the Great, am a detective.
Sometimes I work on cases with
my cousin Olivia Sharp.
She's an Agent for Secrets.
What is an Agent for Secrets?
Olivia will tell you all about it.
She works hard on her cases.
She's here. She's there.
She's everywhere.
She whizzes around the streets
of San Francisco.
Follow her!
I, Nate the Great,
say that you will have
a very good time.

Yours truly,

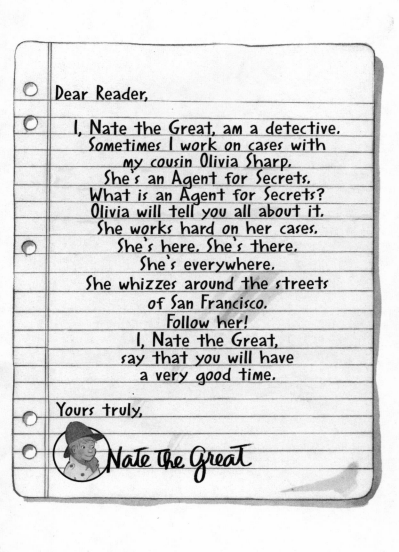

Nate the Great

Olivia Sharp

The Princess of the Fillmore Street School

by Marjorie Weinman Sharmat
and Mitchell Sharmat
illustrated by Denise Brunkus

A YEARLING BOOK

Published by
Yearling
an imprint of
Random House Children's Books
a division of Random House, Inc.
New York

Visit us on the Web! www.randomhouse.com/kids

Educators and librarians, for a variety of teaching tools, visit us at www.randomhouse.com/teachers

ISBN: 0-440-42060-1 (pbk.)   ISBN: 0-385-90291-3 (lib. bdg.)

Reprinted by arrangement with Delacorte Press

Printed in the United States of America

Second Yearling Edition May 2005

10 9 8 7 6 5 4 3 2 1

For Bebe,
who was there from
the beginning and even sooner.
With warm thanks.
—M.W.S. and M.S.

For Queen Avery
—D.B.

Mrs. Fridgeflake Leaves a Note

My name is Olivia Sharp.
I work out of a
penthouse on top of Pacific
Heights in San Francisco.

The penthouse actually belongs to my parents, but right now they're in Europe. I got a letter from them on Saturday. I put it in my IMPORTANT! ANSWER SOON! basket.

Anyway, you get the idea. My parents aren't around much.

I have an owl, Hoot, for company, and a chauffeur, Willie, and a housekeeper, Mrs. Fridgeflake.

And I have my agent-for-secrets business. That means I'm a detective and I specialize in secrets. I'm an agent for secrets.

If you're in trouble, call me.

My first client was Duncan. He answered one of the ads Willie and I put up around town.

My second case began on a school day.

I had just gotten home from school.

I was hungry. I can't stand eating in the school lunchroom. What with the tuna fish sandwiches flying through the air, and the squashed banana that I almost sat on.

I went into the kitchen.

It was empty.

Mrs. Fridgeflake was in her room
watching TV.

But she had left me a watercress
sandwich and a note.

I munched on the sandwich while I read the note.

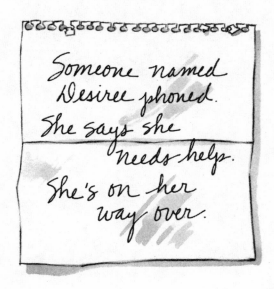

Someone named
Desiree phoned.
She says she
        needs help.
She's on her
     way over.

Desiree. I knew her. She was part of my first case. I had a file on her.

I wondered what she wanted. Could she have a secret to tell me?

chapter two

Little Miss Perfect

I got ready for my new client.

I went to my office. As usual,
Mrs. Fridgeflake had picked up every
speck of dust, fluffed the chair

cushions, and waxed and shined my
red telephone.

I pulled out Desiree's file.

It said, SHE'S PERFECT, NEEDS
HELP BADLY.

I took out a pad of yellow paper,
sharpened two pencils, pulled up

my socks, sat down at my desk, and waited for Desiree.

I didn't have long to wait.

The house phone rang.

It was Willie. "Miss Desiree's here to see you, Boss."

I told Willie to show her in.

A few minutes later there was a knock on my door.

"Come in!" I called.

Willie opened the door and announced, "Miss Desiree."

She looked just as I remembered her. Her face was scrubbed, her blond hair was tied with a rainbow-colored ribbon, her dress was neatly pleated, and her pointy-toed shoes were shiny.

She looked as
if Mrs. Fridgeflake
might have just
dusted and
washed her.

I motioned to her
to sit down.

I sat back in my
chair and waited to
hear Desiree's secret
problem.

Desiree leaned forward and looked me straight in the eye. "I want to be princess of our school," she said.

This was a secret problem?

I glanced at the red telephone on my desk. Maybe it would ring and I would have a real problem to solve.

"I didn't know our school needed a princess," I said.

I made a note to check up on these
things.

"The school doesn't know it, either,"
Desiree said. "Yet."

I crossed out my note.

Desiree smiled. "I have this book, *Princess Faith's Book of Do's and Don'ts.* It tells all about being a princess. I found out that I'm exactly right for the job."

Desiree fluffed her hair.

I was getting curious. "Why do you want to be a princess?"

Desiree stood up. She pulled a piece of paper out of her pocket and started to read:

"BEING A PRINCESS MEANS NEVER HAVING A FROG DROPPED DOWN YOUR BACK.

"BEING A PRINCESS MEANS NEVER HAVING TO EAT LEFTOVERS.

"BEING A PRINCESS MEANS NEVER HAVING TO SLEEP ON A BUMPY

MATTRESS WITH A PEA UNDER IT.

"BUT BEST OF ALL, BEING A
PRINCESS MEANS HELPING OTHERS
TO BE PERFECT
LIKE ME."

"What do you
mean?"

"Watch me,"
Desiree said.

She whipped out
a comb and pulled
and tugged at my
hair. Then she
circled around me.
"Now you're
perfect,"
she said.

Suddenly she bent down and whispered in my ear. "Don't tell anybody about my plan yet. I'm just starting to try it out. I came here to get money for my campaign. May I have ten cents, please?"

I fished in my pocketbook and pulled out a ten-dollar bill instead. Desiree wasn't a real client, but I've got a soft heart for anybody who asks for help.

Desiree looked at the ten dollars and scrunched her nose. "It's wrinkled," she said.

I rang for Mrs. Fridgeflake. When she came I said, "Please iron this ten-dollar bill for Desiree."

As Desiree and Mrs. Fridgeflake left,
Desiree waved good-bye and said,
"Being a princess also means getting to
eat chocolate-covered cherries while
wearing white gloves."

I made some notes on my yellow pad.

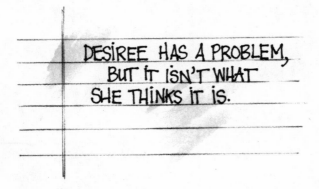

DESIREE HAS A PROBLEM,
BUT IT ISN'T WHAT
SHE THINKS IT IS.

I tore the paper off the pad and put it
into Desiree's file. I closed the file and put
it away.

chapter three
Going Crazy

My red telephone rang.

"Olivia Sharp, Agent for Secrets,"
I answered.

"The world is coming to an end," said

the voice on the other end of the line.

It was Duncan.

I said, "I thought your world-is-coming-to-an-end stuff was gone."

"It was, but it's coming back. Desiree is driving me crazy."

"I thought you wanted her for a friend."

"I did. I do. But she's going around school trying to make everybody perfect.

Today she ordered me to stand up straight.
She polished Sheena's shoes without
asking. And she's trying to give
Mortimer a haircut."

I swiveled around in my chair. I knew
why Desiree was doing these things. It was
part of her secret plan to become a
princess.

Now it was going to be my job to tell her that her plan was bad, bad, bad.

I stopped swiveling. "I'll see what I can do," I said to Duncan.

I hung up.

chapter four

The Secret's Out

I walked out of my office. I went to my furry white chair and sat down. I had some thinking to do.

I looked out at the ships way off in San

Francisco Bay. Sometimes I feel lonely
when I sit in that big chair and look out
that big window. But not that day. I had to
figure out how to stop Desiree from bossing
everybody around. And I wanted to do it
without hurting her feelings.

Things hadn't gone well that day. I had just missed sitting on a squashed banana in the school lunchroom.

I had given Desiree an ironed ten-dollar bill, and she would probably buy more shoe polish with it. Or a horrible-haircut kit.

Some days are good.
And some days
aren't.

But suddenly that day was good!

Because I had just learned from it. *A girl who wants her money ironed would certainly like her school neat and clean!*

I went to my office and called Desiree.

She answered her phone, "Desiree, your future princess."

I could tell this would not be easy.

"Olivia Sharp here," I said. "Why did you answer your phone that way? I thought your plan was a secret."

"It was until you gave me the ten dollars," Desiree said. "Now I can afford to go public."

Things could only get worse.

I said, "It's a really great afternoon for a drive, don't you think? Why don't I come by in my limo and then my chauffeur will zoom us about town in royal style while we talk about your campaign."

"Great," Desiree said.

I rang for Willie to bring the limo around.

chapter five
Princess-in-Waiting

I grabbed my boa and dashed out of the penthouse. I took the elevator down to the street.

As I settled into the backseat of the

limo, I said to Willie, "To Desiree's house and then up and down and around the town."

"Splendid day for a ride, Boss," Willie said.

We rolled out of the courtyard, through the big iron gates, and onto Steiner Street.

Desiree was waiting outside her apartment house.

She was wearing a purple dress, with a bunch of pearls looped around her neck. She also had five bangle bracelets on each arm. And she was carrying a rhinestone purse.

She must have emptied her mother's closet.

Grandly, Desiree stepped into the limo as

if it were hers. As we pulled away from the curb, she smiled at me. She didn't know that I was now operating as Olivia Sharp, Agent for Secrets. She didn't know that I had a plan to help Duncan. And Mortimer. And Sheena.

And come to think of it, myself. I had just noticed that my left shoe was getting scuffed. If Desiree noticed it, I could be next on her list.

chapter six

Does "Oooooo" Mean Yes?

We drove off.

I turned to Desiree and asked, "Since you're running for princess of the school, don't you think you should help the *school*?"

Desiree's face lit up. "The entire school? Every single kid?"

"No," I said. "The school itself. The building. The classrooms. The desks. The blackboards. And above all, the lunchroom. Today, I almost sat on a squashed banana."

"Ooooo," Desiree said. "I could make the school look perfect. Ooooooo."

Was that a yes? I hoped she'd stop bugging the kids and start working on desks and benches and blackboards and walls and floors and windows. A school never needs a haircut or a shoeshine. A school is never told to stand up straight.

I stared at Desiree. At last I knew she was a client. She needed me. This princess

business of hers was getting her into a lot
of trouble.

I opened my pocketbook and peeled off a
hundred-dollar bill. I checked it out to
make sure it looked ironed. "Here," I said.

"Take this and use it for anything you need."

Desiree inspected the bill. Then she said, "I'll spend it on some flowerpots for the halls and classrooms and some soap for the lunchroom, and things like that."

Willie drove us to the Emporium. They
had everything Desiree wanted, except
ironed rags.

When we let her off at her building, Desiree was loaded down with shiny shopping bags. Willie helped her carry them inside.

chapter seven
What Did Hoot Know?

When I got home, I fed
my owl, Hoot. "I've just wrapped up a case,
Hoot," I said to her. Hoot hooted. That
bothered me. I wondered what she knew.

40

I called Duncan.

"I have solved your problem," I said.
"And Mortimer's and Sheena's. Desiree
won't bug you anymore."

"How did you do it?" Duncan asked.

"You'll see," I said. "Now answer this
question: Is the world coming to an end?"

"Not anymore."

"Fine."

I hung up.

I took out Desiree's file.

Desiree wanted to be princess of the
school.

Maybe she'd make it.

Maybe she wouldn't.

But I had done what I could.

I wrote CASE CLOSED.

I put the file away.

The case wasn't really closed, but I didn't know it then.

chapter eight

The Desiree Touch

The next morning I went off to school.

Willie had just left me at the curb when Mortimer came up to me. Mortimer always looks scared. He said, "Duncan told me

that Desiree won't be bugging us anymore.
Is it true? Have you saved my hair?"

"Your hair is safe," I said.

I went into the school.

I didn't expect to see Desiree because she's not in my class.

But I did see a flowerpot near the drinking fountain. I saw it after I stumbled over it. And a folded napkin was hanging neatly from a ring next to the fountain.

It was obvious that Desiree had been there. What else had she done?

chapter nine

A Most Important Call

An hour after I got
home from school, my
red telephone rang. I was in my
bedroom, polishing my left shoe.

I rushed into my office and picked up the receiver.

"Olivia Sharp, Agent for Secrets," I answered.

"Olivia?"

I heard a deep voice. A grown-up was calling me! I grabbed my pencil.

"This is Mr. Baybreath, the principal of your school."

I already knew what Mr. Baybreath's job was. What I didn't know was why he was calling me.

"I have a problem," he said. "Can you come over to the school right away?"

I had already been there once that day. But a case is a case.

"I'll be right over," I said.

I rang for Willie. I grabbed my boa.

"Back to school!" I said to Willie as I climbed into the limo.

"Didn't you learn enough today, Boss?" he asked.

"There's always more to learn," I said.

The fact was, I could hardly wait to find out what Mr. Baybreath wanted!

chapter ten

The Handshake

When we got to school, I went straight to Mr. Baybreath's office.

He was sitting behind his desk. His desk was almost as big as mine.

"Sit down, Olivia," he said.

I sat down opposite him.

"I saw your ad, Agent for Secrets, on the school bulletin board," he said. "I need your help for a problem in this school."

I felt important. The school principal needed me!

Mr. Baybreath leaned across his desk.

I leaned toward him.

He was a principal.

I was his agent.

We were equals.

He said, "Desiree told me that she's running for princess of this school. We don't have any rules against that. We don't have any rules for it, either."

Mr. Baybreath cleared his throat. "However, this morning Desiree started a campaign to clean up the school. She washed the blackboards in five classrooms even before the day's lessons had begun. She put flowerpots on windowsills and they fell crashing to the floor. She painted some of the benches in the lunchroom. Mortimer sat on

one and got paint all over the seat of his pants.

"His mother is very mad. Bare blackboards, crashing flowerpots, painted pants, mad mothers—nothing is safe, no one is safe. And *that's* against the rules!"

Mr. Baybreath fingered his necktie. "I can tell Desiree to stop, but perhaps *you* can do it better."

I squirmed in my chair.

How much did Mr. Baybreath know?

I now knew I had given Desiree a rotten idea along with one hundred and ten dollars in wrinkle-free bills.

Sometimes money buys trouble.

I stood up.

"I'll do my best," I said.

I shook hands with Mr. Baybreath, gave him one of my business cards, and left his office.

chapter eleven
Believe Me, Your Highness!

I went straight home and reopened my file on Desiree.

I wrote:

HOW CAN I TELL
DESIREE TO STOP DOING
SOMETHING I TOLD HER
TO START DOING?

THINK!!!

THINK!!!

I put the file away
and called Desiree.

"We have to go
to the school,"
I said. "Right
now."

"I've already gone to school today," Desiree said.

"You have to go back," I said. "Believe me, Your Highness, you have to go back. I'll pick you up."

"All right," Desiree said.

I was getting tired of going to school. Three times in one day!

I rang for Willie and grabbed my boa, and a few minutes later we were on our way.

"To Desiree's and then to school," I said.

"School again, Boss?" Willie said. "Still learning, huh?"

chapter twelve

No Towers, No Turrets

We picked up Desiree. When we reached
the school, Desiree and I got out of the limo.

"Don't move!" I said. "Stand here and
tell me what you see."

"I see my beautiful drawing of a tulip in the third window of the second floor."

"Forget your drawing," I said. "Just look at the building. Does it have any towers or turrets?"

"No, but it has a playground and a nice sign that says FILLMORE STREET SCHOOL."

"Right," I said. "Is it a palace or a castle or wherever princesses hang out?"

"No."

"So far, so good," I said.

I pulled Desiree inside the school before
she could say anything else.

"This way," I said.

I led her down the corridors until I saw
the principal's office up ahead.

"Tell me what you see," I said.

"I see the principal's office,"
Desiree answered.

"What does the principal do?" I asked.

"He's in charge of the school,"
Desiree said.

"Exactly," I said. "When a school has a principal, it doesn't need a princess, too."

"Oh?"

"Besides, trying to be a princess made you very bossy."

Desiree looked at me wide-eyed. "Bossy?" she said. "I didn't want to be bossy. I just wanted to be perfect."

"You can't be both," I said. "Choose."

"I choose perfect."

"Good choice."

Desiree looked sad. "But it isn't easy to lose a kingdom," she said.

"Cheer up," I said. "We still have one more stop to make."

chapter thirteen

Fit for a Princess

I pulled Desiree back to the limo.

"To the Regal Costume Shop," I whispered to Willie.

When we got there I rushed inside.

I was back in a few minutes with a package. I handed it to Desiree. "Even if you can't be a princess," I said, "you can still *feel* like one."

Desiree opened her package.

"Oh, what a beautiful crown!" she said. "I'll just wear it at home and for special occasions."

Desiree held her crown on her head
while Willie drove us to her building. When
we got there, she stepped out of the limo,
turned, smiled, and curtsied.

chapter fourteen

Keeping in Touch

Willie and I drove home. I went straight to my office and took out my file on Desiree.

I wrote:

CASE
REALLY CLOSED.

I put Desiree's file away.

I wrote a long letter to my parents. I told them everything. Well, almost everything. My parents aren't really interested in tuna fish sandwiches flying through the air and a squashed banana.

Then I started a letter to my cousin Nate the Great.

Olivia Sharp
PACIFIC HEIGHTS, SAN FRANCISCO

DEAR NATE THE GREAT,

HAVE YOU EVER HAD A PRINCESS FOR A

CLIENT? I ALMOST HAD ONE AT SCHOOL.

LET ME TELL YOU ABOUT HER. . . .